ELLA SARAH GETS DRESSED

Margaret Chodos-Irvine

HARCOURT, INC.

San Diego   New York   London

www.HarcourtBooks.com

Library of Congress Cataloging-in-Publication Data
Chodos-Irvine, Margaret.
Ella Sarah gets dressed/Margaret Chodos-Irvine.
p. cm.
Summary: Despite the advice of others in her family, Ella Sarah persists in wearing the striking and unusual outfit of her own choosing.
[1. Clothing and dress—Fiction. 2. Individuality—Fiction.] I. Title.
PZ7.C446255El 2003
[E]—dc21 2002005097
ISBN 0-15-216413-8

C E G H F D

Manufactured in China

The illustrations in this book were created using a variety of printmaking techniques on Rives paper.
The display lettering was created by Margaret Chodos-Irvine and Judythe Sieck.
The text type was set in Goudy Sans Bold.
Color separations by Bright Arts Ltd., Hong Kong
Manufactured by South China Printing Company, Ltd., China
This book was printed on totally chlorine-free Enso Stora Matte paper.
Production supervision by Sandra Grebenar and Pascha Gerlinger
Designed by Margaret Chodos-Irvine and Judythe Sieck

For my own Ella Sarah
—M. C.-I.

One morning, Ella Sarah got up and said,
"I want to wear my pink polka-dot pants,
my dress with orange-and-green flowers,
my purple-and-blue striped socks,
my yellow shoes,
and my red hat."

Her mother said,
"That outfit is too dressy.
Why don't you wear your nice
blue dress with matching socks,
and your white sandals?"

But Ella Sarah said, "No.

I want to wear my pink polka-dot pants,

my dress with orange-and-green flowers,

my purple-and-blue striped socks,

my yellow shoes,

and my red hat."

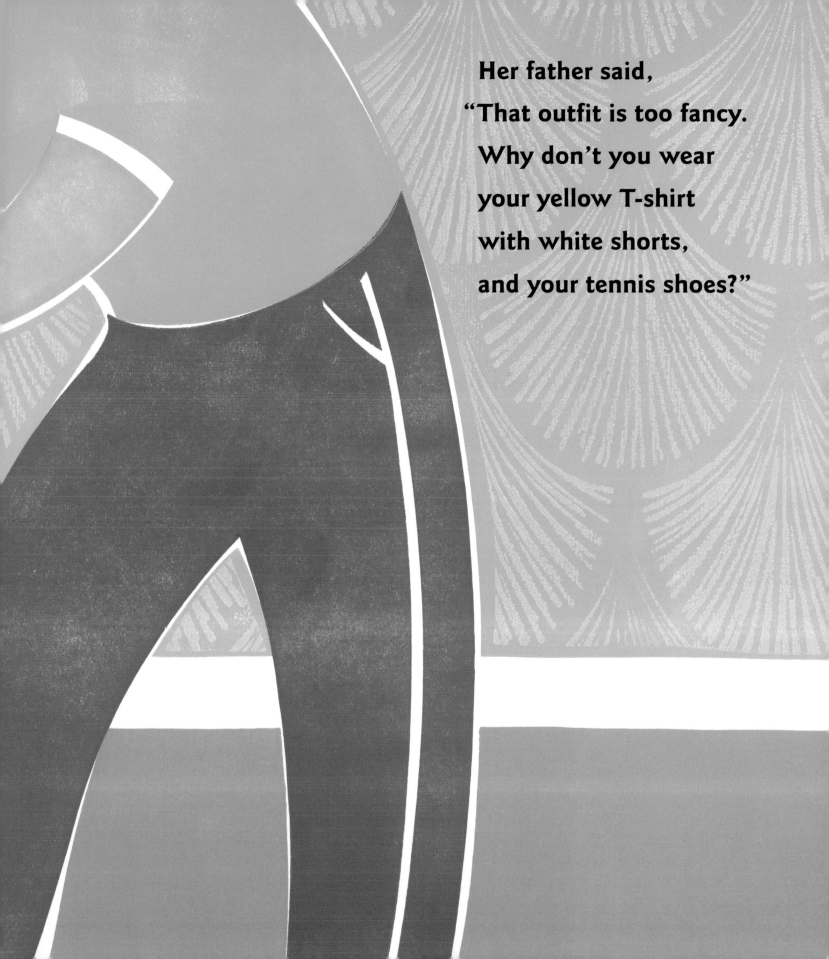

Her father said,
"That outfit is too fancy.
Why don't you wear
your yellow T-shirt
with white shorts,
and your tennis shoes?"

But Ella Sarah said, "No!
I want to wear my pink polka-dot pants,
my dress with orange-and-green flowers,
my purple-and-blue striped socks,
my yellow shoes,
and my red hat!"

Her big sister said,
"That outfit is too silly.
You should wear these overalls
that are too small for me,
and my old boots."

But Ella Sarah said, "NO!

I want to wear my pink polka-dot pants,
my dress with orange-and-green flowers,
my purple-and-blue striped socks,
my yellow shoes,
AND MY RED HAT!"

So…

she put on her pink polka-dot pants,

her dress with orange-and-green flowers,

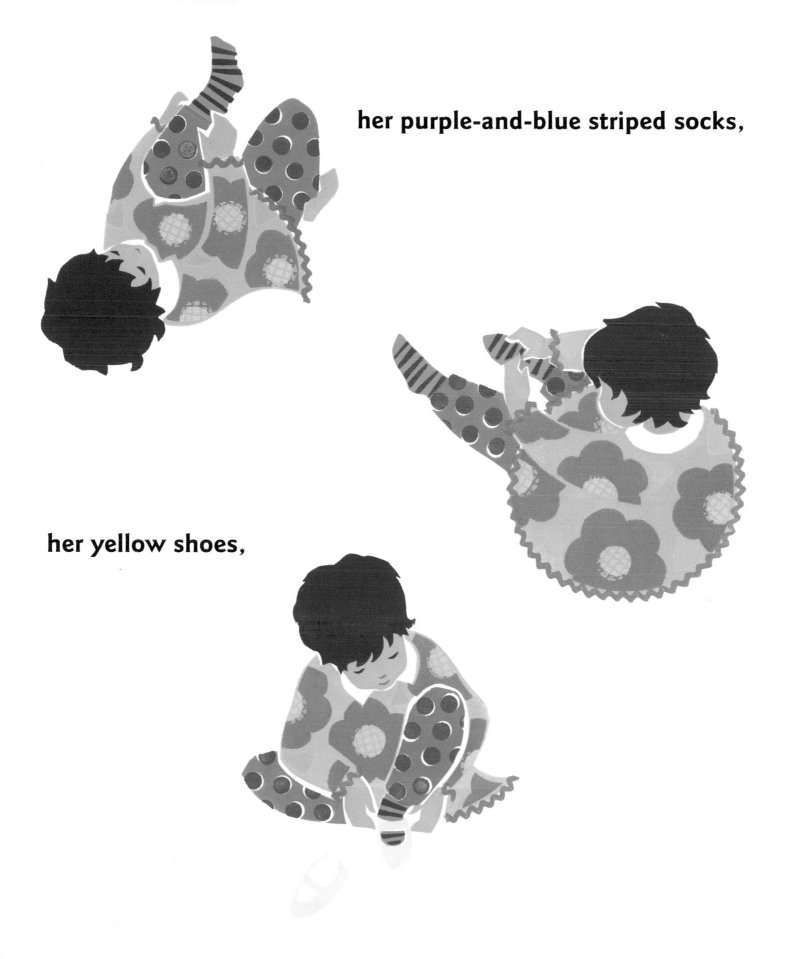

her purple-and-blue striped socks,

her yellow shoes,

and her red hat.

Ella Sarah thought her outfit was just right.

DING
DONG!

And so did her friends.